TABLE OF CONTENTS

Chapter 1

ACK IS BORED

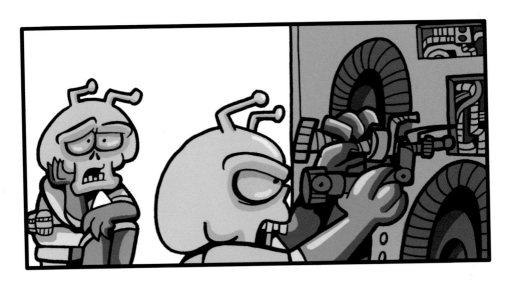

As Eek worked on his spaceship,
Ack looked sad.

"What's wrong?" Eek asked.

"I'm bored," Ack replied.

"You could help me," Eek said.

"Then we could conquer Earth."

"No way!" Ack said. "The last time we tried that, we got sucked into a black hole."

"But nothing bad happened," Eek said.

"It felt like we were flushed down a toilet," Ack said. "I was sick for a week!"

"Fine," Eek grumbled. "What do you want to do?"

"Hmm," Ack thought for a moment. "I want a pet."

"Like a pet earthling?" Eek asked.

"No, no. I want a pet we can teach to do tricks," Ack said. "Like to sit or fetch comets."

"Yeah, earthlings aren't clever enough to learn tricks like that," Eek said.

"Do you think Mum would buy us a pet?" Ack asked.

"Probably not," Eek said. "She's still mad at us for breaking Dad's asteroid bowling trophy."

"Oh, yeah," Ack said. "We shouldn't have tested our rocket packs in the house."

Chapter 2

EEK HAS A PLAN

"I have a plan!" Eek said suddenly. Eek was always planning something.

"I hope this isn't another plan to conquer Earth," said Ack. "Those never work."

"No, and this plan will work," Eek said. "But first, what type of pet do you want?"

"You said Mum won't buy us a pet," Ack said.

"I don't plan on asking Mum for a pet," Eek said. "I plan on making you a pet instead."

Ack wasn't sure what kind of pet he wanted.

"Three-eyed burplers are good at tricks," Eek said.

"Burplers are cool. How do you make one of those?" Ack asked.

"First, we drink lots of Solar Cola," Eek said. "Then we burp into a huge balloon, and—"

"But what if the balloon pops?" Ack asked. "I'm afraid of loud noises."

"Okay, would you like a robot?"
Eek asked. "I have some spare
parts from my spaceship."

"No, robots like to do
maths," Ack said. "I'm afraid of
subtraction."

"That's silly!" Eek said. He shook his head. "How about a goober beetle instead?"

"No, no, never!" Ack yelled. He shook with fear. "I'm afraid of goober beetles!"

"Why?" Eek asked.

"I have one stuck up my nose," said Ack.

Eek looked up Ack's nose. "I can't see anything in your nose," he said.

"Maybe it's gone now, but I still don't want one," Ack said.

"Fine," Eek said. "I'm going to make you a pet that won't be loud, do maths, or get stuck up your nose. Come on!"

Chapter 3

ACK GETS A PET

Eek and Ack zoomed around space, using rocket packs for power. Eek held on tight to a jar of snottle bugs.

"I caught another one!" Ack said.

"Put it in the jar," Eek said.

"Okay, but why are we catching all these snottle bugs?" Ack asked.

"I'll tell you later," Eek said. He flew off. "Just keep looking. We need about a million of them."

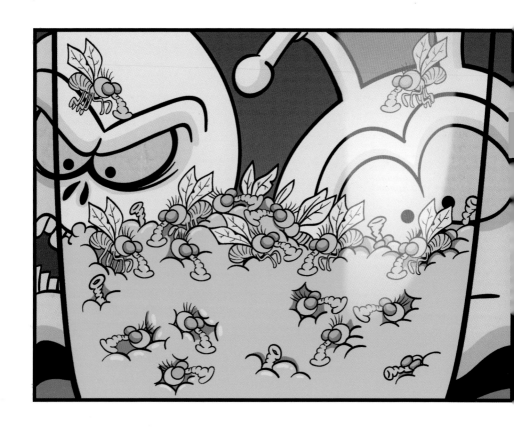

Finally the boys caught enough
snottle bugs. Eek showed Ack
his plan.

"I loaded my slimer with all of
those snottle bugs," he said.

He started the slimer machine. "When the bugs move through my slimer, I'm going to squeeze the snot out of the snottle bugs," Eek said. "Your new pet will plop out of the other end of the slimer!"

"Here it comes!" said Eek.

"He's getting bigger!" Ack shouted.

The pet hugged Ack's leg. "He likes me! He likes me!" Ack shouted.

"I think your new pet is sliming all over your leg," said Eek.

"That's a great name!" said Ack. "I think I'll call him Slimy!"

ABOUT THE AUTHOR

Blake Hoena has written more than 20 books for children. He once spent a whole weekend just watching his favourite science-fiction films. Those films made him wonder if he could invent some aliens who had death rays, hyperdrives, and clever equipment, but still couldn't conquer Earth. That's when he created the two young aliens Eek and Ack, who play at conquering Earth just like earthling children play at beating villains.

ABOUT THE ARTIST

Steve Harpster has loved to draw funny cartoons, mean monsters, and goofy gadgets ever since he first starting using a pencil. At school, he preferred drawing pictures for stories rather than writing them. Steve now draws funny pictures for books as his job, and that's really what he's best at. Steve lives in Ohio in America and has a sheepdog called Doodle.

GLOSSARY

asteroid a large space rock

black hole an area in space that sucks in everything around it

comet a bright, heavenly body that develops a cloudy tail as it slowly moves around the sun in a long, slow path

conquer to defeat and take control of an enemy; Eek always wants to conquer planet Earth.

earthling a creature from the planet Earth

grumbled complained about something in a grouchy way

snottle bug a slime-filled insect that can be found on planet Gloop

three-eyed burpler a lizard-like creature found on planet Gloop that is good at tricks

TALK ABOUT THE STORY

1. Eek and Ack are brothers. Do you think one of the alien brothers behaves better than the other? Explain your answer.

2. Do you think Eek and Ack's mum is going to let them keep Slimy? Why or why not?

3. Would you want Eek to make a pet for you?

WRITING TIME

1. Make up a pet of your own. Describe what it looks like and what things you can do with your pet.

2. Ack is afraid of goober beetles. Write about something you are afraid of.

3. Imagine that Eek and Ack got a pet that is found on Earth, like a dog or a cat. Write a story about them with their new Earth pet.

EXPLORING THE UNIVERSE
with Eek & Ack

Eek wanted to build Ack a pet robot, but Ack was afraid of the subtraction that the robot might want to do. Did you know that robots can do a lot more than just maths? Earthlings have been using robots to explore outer space for more than 50 years.

Robots first landed on the moon in 1966. The Surveyor spacecrafts were sent there to explore whether it was safe for earthlings to land on the moon. Some of these spacecrafts had robotic arms to test how soft the soil was.

In 1977, robots were sent to explore other planets. Voyager 1 and Voyager 2 flew by Jupiter, Saturn, Uranus, and Neptune. They took pictures of the planets.

THE *FUN* DOESN'T STOP HERE!

DISCOVER MORE AT...
WWW.RAINTREEPUBLISHERS.CO.UK